Superstar Secrets

Adapted by M. C. King

Based on the series created by Michael Poryes and Rich Correll & Barry O'Brien

Part One is based on the episode, "Achy Jakey Heart, Part I," Written by Douglas Lieblin

Part Two is based on the episode, "Achy Jakey Heart, Part II," Written by Andrew Green

DISNEP PRESS

New York

HANNAH MONTANA

PART ONE

Chapter One

It wasn't often that Miley Stewart had a Saturday afternoon off. That's because Miley wasn't just an everyday Malibu high school student. She was also secretly Hannah Montana, one of the biggest pop stars in the world.

So on weekends, Miley was usually booked. *Way* booked. There were concert dates, in-store promotional events, and guest appearances on TV. It was one major drawback of being talented, fabulous, and internationally known.

So on Saturday morning, when her dad popped his head in her room to say that their day of meetings had been canceled, Miley gleefully hopped out of the makeup chair.

Miley deserved a day off, or what she called a Regular Girl Saturday. And today was the perfect day for one: blue skies, warm air. If Miley had been dating someone, she'd probably have called him. Maybe they'd have gone to the movies, or just chilled on a quiet section of the beach. But Miley hadn't been interested in anyone—at least seriously—since Jake Ryan, her gorgeous blonde classmate. And that was practically six months ago.

Jake was also famous—a star on TV— who'd seemed crazy full of himself at first.

Miley had thought he was a jerk. But then, after Hannah Montana guest-starred on his show *Zombie High*, the two had actually connected. Jake had admitted that he had a crush on a girl at school: Miley! Then Miley had started to realize that she had a crush on him, too, at which point the two *really* connected—as in kissed! Then Jake broke the news that he was going to Romania for six months to shoot a movie, leaving Miley in the dust—or at least the fine, warm Malibu sand.

Of course, Miley understood that Jake had to leave for work. It was a giant movie role in the big-budget spectacular *Teen Gladiators and the Sword of Fire*; it would change the course of Jake's career. He couldn't turn it down. But it didn't make it any easier for her. Not one little bit.

* * *

In the absence of a boyfriend, Miley's ideal partner for a Regular Girl Saturday was her best friend, Lilly Truscott. Lilly was one of the few people who knew Miley's secret identity. She understood how badly Miley needed a break, and she arrived at Rico's snack bar at the beach prepared for a perfect, stress-free afternoon. She'd loaded up her MP3 player with their favorite music; she had two sets of headphones, a ton of sunscreen, and a pile of the latest fashion magazines. She'd also snuck in a couple of celebrity tabloids — Lilly was a sucker for gossip.

"Lilly, why do you read that tabloid trash?" Miley asked between sips of strawberry-pomegranate smoothie. "They're nothing but lies."

Lilly read aloud from the magazine: *"Hannah Montana looks fabulous. . . ."*

Oh, thought Miley, well, in that case! "With the occasional glimmer of truth," she quipped.

"Uh-oh," Lilly said, turning to the next page.

"Let me guess," Miley said, rolling her eyes. "It's another article about Jake Ryan, isn't it?" This was another reason she didn't like reading tabloids. Jake's star was on the rise, so these days he was all over the gossip pages.

Lilly's voice turned unexpectedly solemn. "It says his movie is done and he's back in town for the premiere."

It took a moment for Miley to absorb Lilly's words.

Jake was back. Jake was back! She didn't know what to feel: excited, because she might see him soon; bitter, because he hadn't even bothered to call her; or downright furious, because he'd kissed her, then ditched her! (Her uncle Earl had words for boys who did that, and they weren't polite ones.) She decided to go with downright furious.

"Big whoop," she said defiantly. "I don't need some guy who kisses me knowing he's about to leave for six months to do some stupid movie."

A strange whooshing noise came up from behind her, but Miley was too absorbed in her angry thoughts to turn around and look. She just kept complaining. "Jake could fall out of the sky wearing a tuxedo and I wouldn't care."

"Uh, Miley?" Lilly had a funny look on her face, and there was an uneasiness in her voice. But Miley continued her tirade. "I'm serious. He could come down and give me a dozen roses and it would make no difference. Zero. Zilch. El zippo."

Lilly's eyes grew wide. "What if he got down on his knees and begged you to take him back?" she asked.

Boy, sometimes Lilly could be really naive. "Yeah, like that's ever gonna happen," Miley cracked.

Lilly pointed down.

What? Had Miley stepped in gum? She glanced at her feet. Nope, her flip-flops were clean. But then, out of the corner of her eye, Miley spied something strange: the well-polished tip of a man's dress shoe. She spun around, confused.

Before her knelt Jake Ryan. A rumpled parachute lay on the ground behind him. Miley wondered if she was seeing things. What had been in that smoothie, anyway? Her eyes darted from Jake's perfectly fitted black suit to the long-stemmed rose in his hand. "Sorry it's only one rose," he said, offering it to her. A grin spread across his handsome face.

Part of Miley wanted to get swept up in the moment. She wanted to take the rose and throw her arms around Jake, kiss him, even. Except, thinking about kissing him made Miley remember what had happened the last time they locked lips. He'd left her! And that was when the other part of Miley—the proud part, the part that didn't let a guy walk all over her—won out.

She regained her composure. "Jake," she cooed in her sweetest possible voice. "I don't know what to say. So I guess I'll just show you how I feel." She picked up her strawberry-pomegranate smoothie and slowly dumped it over Jake's expertly highlighted head.

Then Miley stomped off. So much for her Regular Girl Saturday.

Chapter Two

The doorbell rang at the Stewart house. Miley opened the front door and greeted the delivery man from Malibu Gifts with the usual smile. After all, this was his fifth visit of the day. She signed her name, handed him back his clipboard, then shook her wrist, which ached from so much signing. "Thanks," she said weakly, taking the mammoth basket. She peered underneath the mound of cellophane. Great, just what she needed: another California orange "Will you ever forgive me?" balloon combo.

She set it down next to the giant flower arrangements and canisters of caramel corn. The living room was filled with baskets and flowers from Jake. Each one had a card reading "I'm sorry."

"This has got to stop," Miley grumbled.

"I agree," Mr. Stewart grunted through a mouthful of macadamia-nut cookie. He was sitting on the couch, surrounded by baskets of freshly baked goods. "Either date this Jake boy or tell him to send a workout tape, 'cause I'm about one muffin away from my easy-fit jeans."

Then the front door opened, and Lilly walked in, bearing more gifts from Jake. Apparently, a bunch had been left in the driveway. Grinning, Lilly scoped out the contents of Miley's living room and soon spied something she couldn't resist. "Oooh, peanut-butter balls!"

Miley rolled her eyes. All Lilly and Mr. Stewart cared about was eating! Had they forgotten whom they were dealing with here? "Hello? Guys!" Miley said, raising her voice to be heard over the loud crunching sounds coming from their mouths. "This jerk hurt me, and he's not gonna win me back with peanut-butter balls!"

"Okay, you're right, darlin'," her dad conceded. "We'll get rid of everything." He eyed a basket from the Malibu Prime Meat Company. "I'll start by grilling up these perfectly marbled T-bones."

Lilly looked from Mr. Stewart to Miley to the steak.

"Medium-rare, please," Lilly called.

"You got it," Mr. Stewart answered as he headed out back to fire up the barbecue.

"Come on, Miley," Lilly pleaded. "The poor guy's done just about everything a girl could want. What more can he do?"

"Yeah, Miley. What else can I do?"

Miley's eyes popped open. The voice was male, but it certainly didn't belong to her dad or her brother, Jackson.

She turned to the front door. Standing in the entry was a . . . knight in shining armor?

Miley watched as the knight heaved himself into the room, then lifted his heavy metal helmet to reveal his face. It was Jake.

At the sight of his mussed hair and flushed pink cheeks, Miley felt her anger soften. "You're never gonna stop, are you?" she asked, shaking her head.

He lurched forward, his armor creaking. "You've dumped stuff on me, you've yelled at me, but the one thing you haven't done is tell me you don't care about me. Tell me that and I'll go away," he said.

Miley didn't know how to respond.

But apparently Lilly did. "No! You can't!" she yelled at Miley.

"I know I kissed you and then left," Jake went on plaintively, "and I'm sorry. But I never stopped thinking about you."

"He never stopped," Lilly reminded her.

Miley glared at her to stop. For all she knew, it was just the peanut-butter balls talking.

"I'll go help with the steaks," Lilly said quickly.

"You do that," Miley told her. Then she turned to look at Jake. She took one more deep breath. "Okay," she finally said. After all, who was she trying to kid? "I never stopped thinking about you, either," she admitted.

"Then you'll give me another chance?" Jake asked, smiling.

Miley grinned and nodded. "How about we start with tonight?"

She waited for Jake to look even more thrilled by her answer, but instead, his smile quickly faded. "Ohhhh, uh, slight problem," he said, wincing. "Tonight's my movie premiere."

"That's okay," Miley shrugged. It was kind of cute that Jake thought a movie premiere would be such a big deal to her, when—as Hannah Montana—she'd gone to, like, a million. "It's a little more public than I wanted, but—"

He interrupted her. "No, see, the thing is . . ."

Suddenly, it dawned on her. "You already have a date, don't you?" she said. Of course his whole act had been too good to be true.

"It's not a real date," Jake said quickly,

looking nervous. "It's with my costar. We just have to pretend we're dating for the press. A kiss or two, but it doesn't mean anything."

A kiss or two? A kiss? Or *two*? Miley couldn't believe she'd actually fallen for his whole "I've never stopped caring for you" act! "Nothing you say ever means anything," she declared. "You're the same jerk you were six months ago! Except now you're a jerk with a headache."

And with that, she grabbed a long salami out of one of gift baskets and waved it in the air.

"Oh, no!" he yelped.

Miley beaned him on his metal helmet. "Oh, *yes*!" she yelled.

Chapter Three

Miley wasn't the only Stewart with love issues that day. Her older brother, Jackson, had just laid eyes on the most beautiful girl he'd ever seen. From behind the counter of Rico's, he watched dreamily as she waxed her surfboard.

He couldn't help wondering what it would be like to date her. . . . He became so absorbed in his daydreams, in fact, that he didn't even notice when she packed up her board and walked over.

"I'm so hot," she said, brushing back her silky black hair.

Jackson snapped to attention.

"Yes, you are," he said, gulping.

"Could I get a bottled water?" she asked.

"Yes, you are." Oops. "*Can*. I mean, yes, you *can*," he said, trying to cover his mistake. He reached for a cold bottle. The girl handed him a dollar. "Oh, sorry," Jackson told her. "Rico just tripled his price to three bucks."

The girl looked down at the bottle. "But this is all I have," she said. "And as I said before, I'm so, *so* hot."

Jackson sighed and stared at her. Even her voice was pretty. Jackson couldn't let this beautiful girl go thirsty, even if it meant breaking Rico's rules. He handed her the water. "You can have the employee discount," he said.

The girl smiled in satisfaction—just as her surfboard bag began to wiggle around and unzip itself!

The next thing Jackson knew, Rico was jumping out of the bag and shouting, "You're fired!"

"What are you talking about?" Jackson asked, stunned.

Rico turned to the beautiful girl. "Nice work, Natasha," he said, handing her a dollar. "Go buy yourself something pretty."

Then Jackson watched, forlornly, as the girl walked out of his life forever. *Rico*, he thought, sighing. He'd gotten him. Again.

But it was Rico who was full of accusations. "You ripped me off!" he snarled.

"Me?" Jackson practically laughed. "You're the one ripping people off. Three bucks for a bottle of water? That's stealing!"

"That's America! You want to give stuff away, open your own shack. You can call it IHOF—International House of *Failure*!" Rico replied.

Usually, Jackson took Rico's harassment in stride. After all, he was the boss. Not to mention, a kid who clearly had some issues, as well as a dad who was the owner. Still, three dollars for a bottle of water was wrong. And Jackson didn't appreciate being played, either. As much as he needed a job, he didn't need this one.

In fact, maybe starting his own place wasn't such a bad idea, after all.

"Maybe I will!" he shot back at Rico. "But instead I'll call it International House of Reasonably Priced Water and . . . Fries and Stuff. IHORPWAFAS!"

Chapter Four

That night, Lilly, Miley, and Mr. Stewart sat in the living room. Lilly kept telling Miley to relax, but she just couldn't. She was too angry. She perched on the edge of the couch, fists clenched, jaw tight, eyes glued to the TV. The S-Channel was doing a half-hour special devoted to the *Teen Gladiators and the Sword of Fire* premiere, including live interviews from the red carpet. The *S* in S-Channel stood for *star*.

Though now, as far as Miley was concerned, *S* stood for *slime, scoundrel, smug, simpering, sniveling, sneak, shallow.* She was sure there were other *S* words that described Jake Ryan, too, but she'd have to check the thesaurus later.

The evening's host was Brian Winters. As Hannah Montana, Miley had dealt with him about a thousand times. He was a nice enough guy—though kind of a cheeseball. "And here are the Teen Gladiators," he boomed, grinning. "Jake Ryan and Marissa Hughes, coming over to talk to me."

Miley couldn't look.. But she couldn't *not* look, either. She bit her lower lip and watched as the couple sauntered into the frame. There was Jake with his perfect hair and his ginormous smile, standing arm in arm with the beautiful Marissa Hughes.

Brian Winters turned to Jake first.

"Jake, I don't know what's bigger, the buzz on this movie or the buzz about you two."

"You two!" Miley's stomach churned at the sound of those words.

"Thanks, Brian," said Jake. "We're both really excited about the movie." He looked sweetly at Marissa. "Aren't we, honey?"

Marissa nuzzled up to him. "We sure are, Jakey," she cooed. For a fake couple, Miley thought, they sure looked happy.

"Disgusting," Miley growled.

"Sure is," Mr. Stewart agreed, his eyes half on the TV screen, half on the plate of grilled steak balanced on his knees.

"How can you keep eating that stuff?" Miley asked him. "That's *Jake* steak! It's the *stake* he drove through my heart!"

Her dad nodded slightly as he cut another piece. "Good news is," he said brightly, "it cuts like butter."

"Dad!" How could he be so insensitive? Miley wondered.

"Sorry, Mile," Mr. Stewart said, more seriously. "But you're better off without him. If he's going to choose her over you, he obviously has no taste."

Aw, her dad was sweet.

"Except for meat," Lilly piped in. "This fillet is fantastic!"

Miley glared at her best friend, and then at the TV, where Jake and Marissa Hughes were still acting all lovey-dovey.

"So, Jake, tell me, when did you first know you were in love?" Brian Winters was asking.

Miley leaned in closer. She couldn't wait to hear the answer to *that* one! Jake looked thoughtful for a moment. "I know it sounds hokey, but the minute I looked into Miley's eyes . . ."

25

Lilly and Mr. Stewart nearly choked on their steaks, and Miley's mouth fell open. Had Jake just said what she thought he'd said—on national TV? Or had she merely heard what she wanted to hear?

"Miley?" gasped Marissa. Apparently she'd heard it too. And she didn't look too happy. She glared at Jake.

"Sorry . . ." Poor, confounded Jake sounded shaky all of a sudden. "I meant, *Marissa*."

"Yow!" yelped Brian Winters, clearly thrilled at the scoop he'd just gotten. "Girls hate the name flub. Trust me, been there, done that." He winked. "But we all make mistakes, right, Jake?"

Jake looked serious now. "Yeah," he said softly. "And I'm in the middle of a big one right now." He looked over at his costar and nervously bit his lip. "Marissa's a good friend," he said, "but the truth is, I'm in love with a girl named Miley Stewart. But I blew it. That's the difference between movies and real life." He sighed and lowered his head. "In real life you don't always get a happy ending."

The S-Channel cut to a commercial—and Miley lunged for the remote.

Miley had never been so grateful for anything in her whole, entire life! As she watched Jake say, "I'm in love with a girl named Miley Stewart," for the eight-quadrillionth time, she tried to imagine life before DVRs. It was impossible. How had anyone survived?

I'm in love with a girl named Miley Stewart. Every time Miley watched Jake say the words, she saw something new: the way his lip twitched just a tiny bit; how long his eyelashes were; the way he seemed to be staring right at her when he said her name.

"Mile, you're going to break it," Mr. Stewart warned.

"I don't care," Miley said moonily, pressing REWIND again.

It took Mr. Stewart's confiscating the remote for Miley finally to get a grip. Why watch Jake profess his love on TV, she realized, when she could just as easily watch him do it in person? *Teen Gladiators and the Sword of Fire* was ninety minutes long. She figured the party afterward would be another ninety minutes. If she hurried, she just might make it in time.

Lilly helped her get dressed. They had a hard time choosing between Miley's new blue dress and her purple one. But then they remembered that Marissa Hughes had been wearing blue. Purple it was!

It was a good thing Miley was practically

a pro at putting on makeup. Being Hannah Montana, how could she not be? She did her face while Lilly brushed her hair, helped her with her jewelry, and spritzed her with perfume. Best friends sure came in handy sometimes!

But by the time Miley arrived at the movie theater, the red carpet had been rolled up and the doors were wide open. The velvet rope was gone. Oh, no! Miley thought. Had she missed him?

She stood in the deserted parking lot, wondering what she should do next. Hesitantly, she reached into her bag for her cell phone. Should she call Jake? Text him? That didn't seem very romantic. But just as she pulled out her phone, she saw a lone figure come shuffling out of the theater, his head down. Was it? It was.

Jake.

"Hey, gladiator," she called to him.

"Miley?"

Miley had been thinking about what to say to Jake on the way over and hadn't come up with a thing. But now, face-to-face with him, the words suddenly came to her. She stepped toward him, looked deep into his eyes, and said, "Who says real life doesn't have happy endings?" Then, smiling, she leaned in closer.

If their first kiss had made Miley feel as if time had stopped, this one made her feel as if the stars were shining down on her. It was as though she could actually feel a million lights flashing all around her.

But then she opened her eyes and realized that lights *were* flashing around her—from a million different cameras.

The tabloids! Oh, no!

Chapter Five

It was one thing to see a picture of herself as Hannah Montana in a magazine. That, Miley was used to. It was another thing to see a picture of herself as her real self in a magazine. That was weird. Really weird.

Lilly had arrived at the Stewart house the next morning for breakfast—someone had to eat all of those baked goods!—with an armful of fresh tabloids. Just about every one of them featured an epic pictorial about Miley and Jake's big kiss.

"This is so cool," said Lilly, staring at the *National Inquiry*. The headline read *Jake's New Leading Lady*. "I'm used to Hannah being famous, but now Miley is, too," Lilly said. "Your life is totally going to change."

"It is not," Miley replied. She was positively certain that being in the paper with Jake would just be a minor blip. Tomorrow the tabloids would move on to something else. "Other than having the best boyfriend ever," Miley went on as the doorbell rang and she went to answer it, "my Miley life is going to stay exactly the same."

Then something absolutely bizarre happened. Miley opened the door to find Ashley—as in Amber and Ashley, Miley and Lilly's sworn enemies—standing there, as if it were the most normal thing in the whole world. "Hi, hi!" she said, flashing a grin and walking in.

"Ashley, are you lost?" Miley asked.

"You are so funny," Ashley said, giggling. "I've always loved that about you."

Huh? Miley couldn't have heard right. "Mean girl say what?" she said, flabbergasted.

"Stop it!" Ashley said with an exaggerated laugh. She put her arm around Miley and pulled her so close that their cheeks actually touched. "You are a delight. We are going to be such great friends."

Great friends? Ha! Every year Ashley and Amber put out a Cool List. This year, Miley and Lilly had found themselves on the bottom. Now Ashley was standing in her living room acting as if they were BFFs? Could the day get any stranger?

Apparently, it could. Because not one second later, another unexpected guest suddenly appeared: Amber. "Hi, hi!" she said, merrily skipping in. Then she spotted Ashley, and her face instantly fell. "What are *you* doing here?" she demanded. "You said you were going to the mall."

"You said you were getting a manicure," Ashley snapped in return.

"Yeah. I am," Amber replied, quickly pulling Miley toward her, "with my new BFF!" Her fingernails dug deep into Miley's arm. Ouch!

"You mean *my* new BFF?" Ashley fumed.

Miley shot Lilly a confused and desperate look, and Lilly pointed to the stack of tabloids on the table.

Of course! Miley should have guessed it. Amber and Ashley had found out about her and Jake, and now they wanted to be her friends.

Maybe Lilly was right, Miley realized. If this was any indication, maybe her life really *was* going to change.

Chapter Six

Southern California, in the meantime, not only had a brand-new couple, it also had a brand-new business: Jackson's Shack. Technically speaking, it wasn't really a shack. It was more like a wooden box with a few strips of cardboard glued to the outside. Still, it got the job done.

Jackson had been perfecting his sales pitch all morning, and he was pretty sure he finally had it down pat. "All your beach needs, at reasonable prices!" he called to the passersby as they kept passing by. "I got Mylar balloons, day-old bran muffins. C'mon, everybody, they're nature's broom!"

The only person to stop, however, was Oliver Oken, a loyal friend of Miley's. "Hey, Jackson, how's it goin'?" he asked between bites of a long brown stick of beef jerky.

"I don't get it," Jackson groaned, despondent. He'd set up his business near enough to Rico's that he could see the massive line of people waiting there to be served. "Rico rips people off, and he still gets all the business," he went on.

"Maybe," said Oliver, "it's 'cause at Rico's you can get overpriced hot dogs, and here"—he picked up a bowl of gelatinous green goo—"you get half-priced food poisoning." He took a whiff, then grimaced.

"I mean, seriously, Jackson, this relish stinks."

"That's mayonnaise," Jackson told him. Oliver gulped and clutched his stomach.

But Jackson couldn't help feeling defensive. He'd worked hard all morning on his new business venture, and he was proud of his little place. "Hey, maybe this shack doesn't have refrigeration, and maybe the food isn't exactly edible." He batted a swarm of flies away from the green mayonnaise. "And maybe we do have a bit of a bug problem—but the shack's got character. And, like me, it is here to stay." He pounded his fist on the counter to give his declaration more oomph—but it was a little too much oomph. The weight of his fist made the counter cave in. Then the entire shack collapsed in a splintery mess.

"I can fix this," Jackson said earnestly,

though he didn't sound convincing.

Oliver, meanwhile, had dropped his beef jerky and found it sticking out of a vat of congealed nacho cheese. He frowned bitterly. "You got nacho cheese all over my mom's homemade jerky," he told Jackson.

"How will I live with the guilt?" Jackson replied, rolling his eyes. Couldn't Oliver see that Jackson had much bigger problems than cheesy jerky?

Just then, Jackson's friend Todd arrived. He was a good guy, but not exactly what Mr. Stewart would call "the brightest bulb." He surveyed the mess, then spied the beef jerky. "Hey, what's this?" he asked.

"It *was* my mom's homemade jerky," Oliver explained.

Todd licked his lips. He was famous for being able to eat anything. He didn't ask whether the cheese had been out in the sun all day. And he didn't ask if Oliver had already chewed half of it. He just pulled the jerky from the vat and—to Oliver's horror—popped it into his mouth.

He chewed and chewed. Oliver assumed that at any minute he'd spit it out, but instead he swallowed, then grinned.

"How is it?" Jackson asked, already feeling a little guilty. Todd didn't deserve food poisoning.

But Todd just kept on smiling. *"Mmmmm!"* he said. And he took another bite.

Jackson looked at Oliver. Could it be that if they put their heads together—well, actually, if they put their beef jerky and nacho cheese together—Jackson's Shack might actually have a chance?

Chapter Seven

Miley had never, ever been on a better date before. She and Jake were on a blanket on the beach, staring blissfully up at the night sky. "You see those sparkly stars in a line?" said Jake, pointing. "That's Orion's Belt. And that star, just to the right of the belt? That's my new favorite. It's named Miley."

"Shut up." Miley laughed. "It is not."

"It is now." Jake grinned as he sat up

and reached into the picnic basket. He pulled out a crisp piece of paper with a gold seal at the top. "Here's the certificate to prove it." He handed it to Miley.

"You named a *star* after me?" Miley gasped. Nobody had ever named anything for her before!

"It was either that, or a half mile of Interstate 5," Jake joked. He took her hand. "Miley," he said, "I've never felt so close to anyone. I don't want there to be any secrets between us. So I'm going to tell you something I've never told anyone before."

Uh-oh. The warm, cozy feeling Miley had suddenly got colder. There had to be a catch, she knew. It was all too good to be true. Jake had a secret. Her mind raced through the catalog of awful possibilities: *He was actually thirty years old. He had twelve toes. He still sucked his thumb.* She did a silent prayer: Please don't have twelve toes. She glanced at his feet and looked straight at him, bracing herself for the worst.

Jake looked deep into her eyes. He took a deep breath of salty beach air, then bravely confessed: "My real name is Leslie."

Miley waited for him to say something else. But he didn't. She was confused. "Leslie. Right, that's good. Seriously, what's the secret?"

"That *is* the secret."

Miley had to giggle. She had been worrying for nothing.

"And I love that name!" she said full of relief. "I had a hamster named Leslie until I figured out it was a boy." Oops. She winced.

"Go ahead," Jake groaned. "Make fun."

But Miley hadn't meant to. Not at all. "No, really, I'm sorry," she said. "I'm actually touched that you trust me so much."

Jake looked at her happily and took her hand. "I do," he told her, "and I can't tell you how great it feels that I don't have to hide part of my life from you. 'Cause I know you'd never do that to me."

As the tiny tea lights Jake had placed all around their blanket flickered, the weight of his words landed heavily on Miley: *Hide part of my life. I know you'd never do that.*

"Yeah. Sure," she said, gulping. She fidgeted uncomfortably. Images of Hannah Montana filled her mind. "Of course."

"Now we know everything about each other," Jake said, grinning.

"Yeah. Sure. Of course," Miley said again. Words were failing her.

"And there are no secrets between us," Jake went on.

Miley looked at him and nodded. This was her chance. This was her opening. Now was precisely the time to tell him that she too had a secret . . . and it wasn't a little one like being named Leslie. It was time to tell him right then and there that Miley was already a star. "I'm Hannah Montana!" she wanted to scream. But she couldn't. She just wasn't ready. She just wasn't sure. So instead, she just mumbled, "Yeah. Sure. Of course," again.

Funny, she'd spent so much time wondering if she could trust Jake. Now she knew she could. But could Jake trust *her*?

After their moonlight picnic, Jake and Miley stood outside her front door.

"Well . . ." she began.

"So . . ." said Jake.

"Yup . . ." said Miley. She put her hand

on the doorknob, then pulled it away. Was Jake going to kiss her or not? Or should she, maybe, kiss him? Yeah, she thought, I should, even if she did still feel too weird and guilty to enjoy it.

She raised herself up on her tippytoes and started to lean in. But then she heard a sound . . . the sound of a newspaper rustling. She hadn't even noticed her dad sitting there reading on the porch!

Mr. Stewart never sat out at night. Clearly, he had been waiting up for her.

"Daddy, don't you think the light would be much better in the house?" Miley asked, cocking her head to the left, which was code for "Leave us alone!"

"Don't worry about me, darlin'," Mr. Stewart said, "I can see everything I need to see right here."

Miley glared.

"Oh, all right," he said, relenting. "I'm going to read *The Family Circus*. Should take about two seconds. Ready?" He raised the paper in front of his face. Apparently he wasn't budging.

Jake and Miley moved closer to each other, and Mr. Stewart dropped his paper. "One. Two," he counted. "Good night, Jake."

Jake sighed in frustration, then smiled at Miley. "'Night, sir," he said, waving good-bye.

"Arrrgh!" shouted Miley as she stormed into the house.

Calmly, her dad followed her. "Oh, honey, don't be mad at me. I gave you two seconds. It's not my fault the boy's got slow lips."

"It's not that," she groaned. At least it was not *just* that. "Daddy, tonight Jake was totally honest with me, and because of the Hannah secret, I couldn't be the same with him. What kind of relationship will it be if I have to lie to him about half my life?" Miley paced the living room. She was too upset to sit still.

Then her dad gave her the most unexpected advice. "Well, you could always tell him the truth," he said.

Miley froze in place. Tell him the truth? That was the craziest thing she'd ever heard! Barely anyone knew she was Hannah Montana, and it was crucial to keep her identity as secret as possible. She knew that if anyone blabbed, the normal life she'd worked so hard to have would instantly be gone. She'd never have a Regular Girl Saturday again. Scratch that. She'd never have a Regular Girl *Anyday* again. "What?!" she bellowed.

"Or not." Her dad shrugged. "Honey, it's a tough decision, but I'm sure you'll make the right one."

"No, I won't!" Miley cried, shaking her head in desperation. Just when she needed her dad to butt into her life, he was acting all calm and cool! No fair! "I'm fourteen," she reminded him. "I'm almost guaranteed to mess this up. You're the adult. You're supposed to tell me what to do!"

"What kind of father would I be if I just ordered you around all the time?" her dad asked her innocently.

"A normal one!" Miley shouted. Oh, this was hopeless. "I swear, you are no help at all," she told Mr. Stewart. Then she stomped upstairs to her bedroom.

Chapter Eight

While Miley continued to struggle over her dilemma, a new day dawned at Jackson's Shack—though it wasn't called that anymore. Now it was Jackson & Oliver's Cheeze Jerky. Gone were the bowls of rancid relish and crusty ketchup. No more lukewarm tap water served in paper cups. Now the shack sold Cheeze Jerky.

Not only had Jackson and Oliver streamlined the menu, they had customers now, too.

Eating, breathing, and, most important of all, paying customers. An actual line of them. As Jackson slathered a stick of jerky with cheese, he noticed his ex-boss, Rico, glaring at him from across the way.

Jackson wasn't a petty guy. Still, he couldn't deny the satisfaction this gave him. Every customer who came to Jackson & Oliver's Cheeze Jerky was a customer who didn't go to Rico's. That meant that every dollar Jackson made was a dollar Rico lost. And there was nothing that irked Rico more than a dollar lost.

Jackson also noticed that Natasha, the beautiful girl who'd helped get him fired, was by Rico's side. She was holding a plate of food, probably one of Rico's overpriced hamburgers or hot dogs. He watched as she lifted something from the plate to her lips. Then he nearly fell back in shock.

She was eating Cheeze Jerky!

While Jackson looked on in surprise, Rico's blood was boiling.

Who did these customers think they were, he wondered. Abandoning his place for that . . . that . . . *shack*? Actually, it wasn't even a shack. It was a pile of wood and cardboard manned by his cheating, scheming ex-employee, Jackson, and his partner in idiocy, Oliver. Those guys didn't know a thing about making food or running a business. How dare they!

"Cheeze Jerky?" Rico grumbled. "That's the dumbest thing I've ever heard."

"Maybe," said Natasha, who had taken over Jackson's duties. "But it's delicious."

Rico turned in horror to see her eating Jackson's Cheeze Jerky! Under his roof! Great, now she'd betrayed him, too!

"Just try it," she told him.

Rico stared at the sticky mess of dried meat and processed cheese and wrinkled his nose. No way was he putting that health violation into his mouth. But then something his dad and mentor had once said popped into Rico's brain: to beat the competition, you have to know the competition. Cheeze Jerky was the competition. Rico would do anything in the name of business. He grabbed a piece of Cheeze Jerky and popped it in his mouth.

He had expected salty, stale meat and sticky, clumpy cheese. Boy, was he surprised. The beef was crunchy, yet succulent; the cheese was thick, yet creamy. And the combination of the two—well, not since peanut butter and jelly had there been a better match. Rico chewed for a few more long seconds, then spat the mouthful out onto the ground in a burst of fury.

"You don't like it?" Natasha asked.

"It's delicious," Rico confessed. Natasha looked surprised. After all, it was a rare day when Rico admitted defeat. But then she saw that Rico didn't look defeated at all. He glared at the crowd forming around Jackson & Oliver's Cheeze Jerky, and he rubbed his hands together the way evil masterminds do when they're plotting world domination. "It's not mine . . . *yet*!" All he needed was a little time. . . .

Chapter Nine

Miley had a feeling Jake would call her to do something the next day, and he did. When he told her he couldn't bear the thought of going a day without seeing her, she was touched. He wasn't doing that typical guy thing of pretending to be cool. Which is why she felt so bad when she had to say no. And even worse when she had to lie about why.

Hannah Montana was going to a local

grade school to read to the students. When she told Jake that she had "a school thing," Miley tried to convince herself it wasn't *really* a lie. But she couldn't shake the guilt. What she'd told Jake was only half the truth, at best. He deserved a whole lot more.

Miley didn't believe in magic. But sometimes she thought the blonde wig she wore as Hannah Montana had special powers. Usually, all she needed to do to was put the wig on and presto! She was in Hannah Montana headspace. But this afternoon the wig didn't have its usual mojo. She kept thinking about lying to Jake. She told herself to focus, but it wasn't any use. Though Hannah Montana might have been sitting in a tiny, Play-Doh–spattered chair, surrounded by beaming second graders, Miley Stewart was somewhere else entirely.

It didn't help much that the book the

teacher had chosen for her to read aloud was *Trudy, the Truthful Turtle*. Trudy lived on Honest Island. She told a lie—a super-minor one, as far as Miley could tell—and the other turtles found out, and boy, did they come down on her! Poor Trudy wanted to crawl into her shell in shame. And by the time she got to the end of the book, Miley was about ready to do the same.

"*And so,*" she read from the last page, gritting her teeth, "*all the animals on Honest Island were saved. All because Trudy, the Truthful Turtle promised she would never tell . . . another lie.*"

"Thank you, Hannah!" said the teacher.

"Thank you, Hannah Montana!" shouted the class.

Phew! Miley stood up, anxious to bolt, but the teacher had other plans, clearly.

"Does anyone have questions about honesty for Miss Montana?" she asked.

Questions about songwriting, Miley could answer. Questions about makeup, piece of cake. But questions about honesty? Now? Please! No way.

"Or, we could read another book!" Miley suggested quickly. She grabbed a book out of a girl's lap. "How about"—she winced as she read the title—"*Frankie, the Fibbing Frog*?

"Sweet niblets," she muttered under her breath, tossing the book aside.

A little girl raised her hand. "Hannah," she asked innocently, "have *you* ever lied?"

Who knew such a sweet-looking child could be so . . . evil?

"Good question," Miley said dryly; then she turned her back on the girl. "Anyone else?"

A little boy was waving his hand. He looked like a safe bet.

"Yes?" Miley said.

"Why won't you answer Samantha's question?" the little boy asked. Oooh. He was evil, too!

"Listen . . ." Miley said, desperate to come up with an answer. "Sometimes life is . . . complicated. And people get put into situations that are . . . complicated."

"Miss Montana," the teacher interrupted. She looked unamused. "I'm sure you're not suggesting to a class of second graders that lying is ever okay."

"No, of course not," Miley assured her. "It's just that . . . sometimes you have to."

Miley winced and bit her lip. No sooner had the words left her mouth than she regretted them immensely. Then again, at least she was being honest.

"Hannah Montana's a liar!" shouted the little girl she'd ignored.

"*Ooohhhh!*" cried the class, in unison.

"No!" Miley protested. "Of course not, listen, just listen, it's like, well . . . Superman doesn't tell Lois Lane that he's Clark Kent—but it doesn't mean he doesn't love her."

"Superman's a liar?" cried the little boy.

"*Whoa!*" the kids exclaimed, reeling.

Miley tried her best to comfort them. "Never mind. He isn't real."

"Superman isn't *real*?" someone squealed.

Miley looked around at the classroom full of stricken faces. "Oh, come on," she said, taking one more stab at explaining herself to them. "How many of your parents have said to you, 'You're going to be president someday'?"

They all raised their hands.

"See?" Miley said. "I mean, think about

it: not all of you can be president! Odds are, none of you will be president!"

She grinned, but her smile quickly faded as the classroom was filled with wails. Miley was only too glad when the grim-faced teacher gave her watch an impatient tap. Visit over. At last!

Miley had barely left the school grounds before she called Jake. She had to see him as soon as possible.

She said she'd meet him on the beach, but she didn't bother changing. She put a trench coat on over her Hannah clothes, then took off her wig and slipped it into her inside pocket.

The sun had set and the beach was empty by the time Jake arrived. "Miley, I got your call," he said. "What's up?"

Miley knew that if she wasted time, she

might lose her nerve, so she got straight to the point. "Listen, Jake, you were totally honest with me, so . . . I have a secret, too, and I'm not sure how you're going to take it."

"Oh, come on, how bad can it be?" Jake asked with a laugh. "You're not married, are you?"

"No, I'm not married," said Miley. "And neither is . . . Hannah Montana."

Jake looked puzzled. "What?" he asked, utterly confused.

It was time. Miley turned her back to him. She unbuttoned her trench coat, pulled out the wig, and put it on her head. Then she whirled back around to face him.

"I'm Hannah Montana," she said.

The truth was out. There was no turning back now. . . .

Part One

"Lilly, why do you read that tabloid trash?"
Miley asked.

"Jake could fall out of the sky wearing a tuxedo
and I wouldn't care," said Miley.

There, before Miley, knelt Jake Ryan. A rumpled parachute lay on the ground behind him. Miley wondered if she was seeing things.

"Jake," Miley cooed, "I don't know what to say. So I guess I'll just show you how I feel." Then she dumped her smoothie over his head.

The living room was filled with baskets
and flowers from Jake.

"Then you'll give me another chance?"
Jake asked, smiling.

Miley's mouth fell open. Had Jake just said what she'd thought he said—on national TV?

Miley had never been on a better date before.

Part Two

"Wow, I'm kind of thirsty," Jake said. Instantly, dozens of cups were offered to him.

"I made up the secret so I could go out in the world like a normal person," Miley explained.

Jake announced to the ice cream parlor that he was thirsty, but no one brought him water since he was in disguise.

Miley, Lilly, and Oliver were totally spent. Jake hadn't stopped talking about himself for hours.

"Lilly, you're a genius!" Miley said excitedly. Now she knew how to get rid of Jake.

"Little Miss Hannah Montana can't handle it when it's all about Jake Ryan," Jake said to Miley.

"Being normal is not stupid. It lets me have real friends. And it reminds me that I'm just like everybody else," Miley said.

"No matter what happens, we're going to make it through this," Mr. Stewart said.

Disney

HANNAH MONTANA

PART TWO

Chapter One

Miley's words hung in the cool evening air. "I'm Hannah Montana. . . . I'm Hannah Montana. . . . I'm Hannah Montana. . . ." It had been several minutes since she'd said them, and yet Jake still hadn't replied.

Miley waited. A wave crashed. In the distance, she could hear cars honking on the freeway.

And she waited. . . . A firefly flickered.

And she waited. . . . A seagull swooped down from the sky.

She knew it was a lot to take in. She remembered when Lilly had found out. It seemed very long ago now, but Miley could still remember how shocked she'd been. And what about Oliver? He'd collapsed! They'd literally had to revive him. At least Jake was more composed than Oliver. Though, come to think of it, his complexion had gone a little seaweedy . . .

"Jake?" she said finally. He looked back at her blankly. "Jake?" He barely blinked. Miley was starting to get worried. She tried something else. "Leslie?" she said.

This, at last, seemed to jolt Jake to attention. "Just gimme a second, okay?" he said.

"If it helps," Miley told him, "you're doing better than Oliver. He fainted when I told him."

"Jake Ryan doesn't faint," Jake said, then wobbled from one foot to the other. "Leslie, on the other hand, is a little woozy." He sat down heavily on a rock, and Miley sat beside him.

"Listen," she told him, "if you're gonna be mad, don't be mad at Miley. *She* wanted to tell you, but—"

"But what?" he asked. "*Hannah* wouldn't let her?" Miley noticed with relief that the pink color had returned to his cheeks.

"Well, you know, she's a 'pop star,'" Miley joked. "You know how they can be—total divas. I try to avoid them."

Jake looked at her sideways. "So, it's just the two of you, right? I mean you're not also the Dixie Chicks, are you?"

Miley laughed. "No, just Miley and Hannah. Two chicks here."

Jake nodded. "Well, if that's the case,

then . . ." He took a deep breath, and Miley crossed her fingers. If she hadn't been wearing Hannah Montana's tight high heels, she would have crossed her toes, too. She held her breath while she waited for him to finish. "I think you're both pretty great."

"Really?" Miley exhaled. She happily uncrossed her fingers.

"Really," Jake repeated.

Filled with relief, Miley returned Jake's smile. Honestly, she couldn't believe how well it had gone! Jake was even more awesome than she'd thought. She couldn't wait to throw her arms around his neck and kiss him!

But no sooner had their lips touched than a deafening whirring came from overhead. And then there were the lights. It was just like their last real kiss, outside the movie theater, except that, instead of millions of little flashing lights, there was now just one gigantic spotlight.

Instinctively, Miley and Jake jumped away from each other. They looked up to see that the light was coming from a helicopter. "Oh, man, the paparazzi!" Jake muttered, shaking his fist at the sky.

"They follow me everywhere," Miley explained apologetically.

Jake gave her a funny look. "Uh, I think they're following *me*," he said. "You know . . . big movie about to open?"

Miley raised an eyebrow. Was Jake Ryan competing with Hannah Montana? "Hello. Millions of albums *already* sold?" she reminded him.

"Okay," Jake said, shrugging. "We'll just go ask them, then." He stepped toward the helicopter. What was he going to do, she wondered. Scream up to them?

Then it suddenly dawned on her. She was dressed as Hannah Montana. Yet just yesterday the tabloids had featured pictures of Jake with *Miley*. If they got pictures of him kissing Hannah, he'd look like a two-timing player. "No!" she shouted, grabbing his arm and yanking him back. "You're not dating Hannah, you're dating Miley! You can't get caught cheating on me with me."

"Huh?" Jake was confused.

"Keep up, movie star, this ain't rocket science," Miley teased, giving his hair a playful tousle. There wasn't time for joking, though. They needed to make a move. And fast!

Pulling Jake after her, Miley dashed behind Rico's. When the coast was clear, they hightailed it off the beach.

Chapter Two

Telling Jake her secret was a big deal to Miley. And not just to her, but also to her friends. Lilly and Oliver came over bright and early the next morning to get a recap. They wanted all the details.

"Helicopters, movie stars, forbidden love — it's all so romantic," Lilly said dreamily.

"So, when you told him you were Hannah, he didn't faint?" asked Oliver. "Not once?"

"Nope," Miley replied. "Steady as a rock."

Oliver sighed sadly, still a little sensitive about *his* fainting when he'd heard.

"You know what the best part is?" Miley went on, grinning. "Now I can finally be myself with the guy. No more secrets. Just a normal boy-girl relationship."

She looked up eagerly at the kitchen clock. Eleven in the morning. Only seven hours until she saw Jake again. They were going to the movies. What could be more of a normal boy-girl relationship than that?

Miley was wrong, of course. Going to the movies with Jake Ryan was far from a normal experience, beginning with standing on line for tickets. A manager from the movie theater walked by, noticed Jake, and before Miley knew it, whisked them out of the line. Then, when they tried to pay for the tickets, the manager refused to take their money. Not only that, they got free vouchers to come again another time. It was the kind of special treatment given to celebrities.

But the thing was that, even as Hannah Montana, Miley made a point of always trying to pay her own way. If she'd been in Jake's situation, she would have refused special treatment, paid for herself, and given the free tickets to a couple of kids, who'd have been totally psyched. But Jake didn't protest at all. And then, when the manager personally escorted them into the theater and kicked an older couple out of the two best center seats, Jake didn't complain, either. He just sat down. It seriously bugged Miley. But she told herself that it was all because he didn't want to insult the movie manager.

Then there were the other moviegoers. Miley knew that being around a big movie star was exciting, and it was nice of Jake to sign all those autographs for everyone. But did he have to be *that* nice? Every time Miley tried to start a conversation with Jake, they'd get interrupted.

When the lights finally dimmed and the movie started, Miley expected things to get better. But while she and Jake watched the movie, the rest of the audience watched them! Jake told her to ignore it all, but how could she? All those people waiting to see if she and Jake held hands, or snuck a kiss. It was very distracting. This was not how she had pictured their date at all.

Finally, Miley couldn't take it anymore. She turned around. "Why don't y'all take a picture? It'll last longer," she snapped. The next thing she knew, a sea of camera phones were flashing. "Hello, people!" Miley called out in exasperation. "It's just an expression!"

"Miley," Jake whispered, "relax, just ignore them. Why don't I get us some drinks?"

Miley nodded. Not a bad idea.

But then the oddest thing happened. Jake didn't get up to go to the refreshment stand. Instead, he stayed seated and, in a casual, slightly raised voice, said, "Wow, I'm kind of thirsty." Instantly, dozens of cups were offered to him. Jake turned to Miley. "You want water, fruit juice, or iced tea?"

Miley sank into her seat. At that moment, all she wanted was to disappear.

Miley was quiet for most of the ride home. When Jake asked what was wrong, she shrugged and just said, "Nothing." But something *was* wrong, really. The night had been a disaster. Jake's fans were so aggressive. But it was more than just that. What really bothered Miley was that Jake seemed so into it! As if he thought he deserved all that free stuff. There was nothing she disliked more than stars who thought they deserved special treatment. And as Hannah Montana, she'd met more than her share of them.

Was Jake Ryan not exactly the guy she'd thought he was?

Miley kept reminding herself of how sweet and forgiving he had been when she confessed her secret. And how he'd tried so hard to please her. Which was why, when they got back to Miley's house, she kept her misgivings to herself. After everything he'd done, Jake deserved the benefit of the doubt.

Miley apologized for making Jake leave

the movie early. "But your fans wouldn't leave us alone all night," she explained.

Jake looked surprised. "Come on, fans are just part of the territory. I thought Hannah Montana would be used to that."

Miley shook her head. "*She* is, but Miley isn't. That's the reason I made up the secret," she explained. "So I could go out in the world like a normal person."

Jake nodded. "And that's kind of hard to do when you're dating me," he said.

"A little bit."

They were quiet for a moment, neither of them sure what to say. "Does this help?" Jake asked at last. He leaned forward and gave her the gentlest kiss.

Miley smiled. "A little bit," she said. And as Jake took her hand, all her doubts seem to melt away.

Chapter Three

No doubt about it. Jackson & Oliver's Cheeze Jerky was a certified hit! The guys were selling the stuff faster than they could make it. Customers lined up for seconds. Even thirds!

Of course, they knew their success hadn't escaped Jackson's old boss Rico's eagle eyes. They'd seen him staring vulturelike from across the sand. They knew he'd stop at nothing to steal their business out from under them.

So, later that day, Jackson and Oliver were immediately suspicious of the older woman who kept going on and on about the wonders of Cheeze Jerky. She was lingering just a little too long. She was also pushing an extralarge stroller with a giant, oddly wrapped baby.

"Sonny, this Cheeze Jerky is fantastic!" the woman gushed. "You have to give me the recipe."

Oliver decided to go ahead and take the bait. He pulled a worn slip of paper from his pocket and waved it tauntingly in the air. "Oh, sorry, ma'am," he said, ever so politely. "My mom's jerky, and his dad's cheese recipe?" He nodded over to Jackson. "They're top secret."

"But I'm a grandmother. You can trust me," the woman said.

Jackson stepped up and smiled at her sweetly. "You know, we would . . . but we weren't born yesterday. And neither was this baby!" And with that, he whipped the blanket off the giant stroller. The customers gasped. The baby was not only freakishly large, he was sucking on a pacifier while simultaneously growling. It was Rico! "Cootchy-cootchy-coo!" Jackson teased, tickling his old boss under the chin.

Rico pulled the pacifier from his mouth with an angry *pop!* "This isn't over! That Cheeze Jerky will be mine!" he cried with a demonic laugh. "Mwa-ha-ha-ha! *Vámonos, abuela,*" he ordered the old lady. And he glared hotly at Jackson and Oliver as she wheeled him away.

Jackson and Oliver watched. They were amused for now. But they'd have to watch their backs, they knew, not to mention their Cheeze Jerky.

Later that day, Oliver left Jackson in charge of the jerky so he could meet Lilly and Miley and Jake at Pizza Bytes. They had been craving the Mushroom-Meatball Spectacular Deep-Dish Surprise. And apparently, they weren't the only ones.

"Oh, man, it's packed," Miley said, as she worked her way through the mob of pizza-lovers. "This is going to be a disaster," she said, catching her breath and looking around. There was barely an empty table in the place. She'd been looking forward to hanging out with Jake and her other friends. But how would they ever get any privacy?

Lilly shrugged, her mind on past pizza endeavors. "If Oliver orders the chili-dog pizza again, we'll just sit by the window."

"Stop worrying about Oliver," Miley told her. "I'm thinking about *Jake*. No matter where we go, it's like a zoo. The beach, the movies, the mall—everybody just does *this*." Miley got up close to Lilly, craned her neck so her head jutted out, then widened her eyes and stared.

"Okay, that's creepy," Lilly said. She paused for a moment, examining Miley's right eye. "And by the way, easy on the liner. Lookin' a little . . ."

Suddenly, a boy behind them spoke up. "She looks very nice to me." He had a strange foreign accent that Miley couldn't quite place. She took in his jet-black hair and gigantic sunglasses. Yuck, thought Miley. Sunglasses indoors. So wannabe!

"Thanks," she said in a tone that was polite but distant. "Appreciate it, but I have a boyfriend." Then she turned back around. Conversation over.

Apparently, however, the guy didn't get the message. "Big coincidence," he drawled, "'cause I have an American girlfriend. And her name is *Miiiiley.*"

Miiiiley??? She spun back around. "Weirdo, say what?" she said.

The guy lifted his glasses from his eyes for a second, then lowered his voice and whispered, "Miley, it's me," in perfect English. Now *that* voice was familiar.

"Jake?!" Miley said.

"*Shhh!*" he said, putting on the accent again. "It's Milos. You like?" He grinned at her stunned expression, then slipped back into a normal whisper. "Look, now I'm just a regular guy. I'm a nobody. Like Oliver." He nodded toward Miley's friends.

"Brilliant," said Oliver, looking Jake's

disguise up and down. Then he processed the minor insult. "Hey!"

Miley ignored Oliver. "You did this for me?" she asked Jake.

"I did this for *us*," Jake explained.

Miley thought about how just the night before she'd questioned Jake's character. Now she looked at him in his big glasses and funny wig and felt guilty. Jake *did* want to be a normal person. "You're so sweet," she told him. "But could you please be sweet without the accent?" She didn't want to hurt his feelings, but it was a little weird.

"If it makes you happy, sure," Jake said with a shrug. "I'm just a normal guy, with normal friends, eating normal pizza."

Miley sure liked the sound of that — except that they weren't eating pizza. They were still standing in line, a line that was barely moving.

Miley kept looking at the clock. Lilly kept rubbing her hungry stomach. Jake stamped his foot in frustration. Finally, he'd had enough.

"Excuse me, people, I'm ready to order!" he called as he pushed through the crowd toward the counter.

"Hey, buddy, who do you think you are?" asked one angry guy. As far as he could see, Jake was just a rude guy with thick black hair and eighties shades.

Jake grinned. "Well, actually, I'm J—"

Miley swooped in to finish Jake's sentence: "Just a normal guy!" She smiled as she pulled Jake back, then whispered, "And here in Normalville, we take a normal number and wait our normal turn."

Jake pursed his lips and nodded. "Right. No sweat. I did this in an episode of *Zombie High:* 'Haunted Deli: Take a

Number and Wait . . . to Die.' So, uh, what number are we?"

"Thirty-two," Oliver told them.

The counter guy called for number six.

Jake's mouth fell open. "Are you kidding me?" he groaned loudly.

"Milos!" Miley scolded.

"Oh, sorry," Jake said. "Got it. Normal people wait. I'll wait." But barely a minute went by before he was complaining again.

"This is endless!" he exclaimed bitterly, turning on his heel to leave. "Let's go!" And before Miley or anyone else could stop him, he stormed out the door.

"Looks like Milos has a bit of a temper," Lilly remarked with a little eye roll.

Miley had to agree. In fact, she thought, that was kind of an understatement.

Miley and her friends decided to ditch the

pizza place and follow Jake. They'd all go out for ice cream instead. It wasn't exactly dinner fare, but it was the only place where they wouldn't have to wait in line. Miley didn't want Jake to freak out again.

Still, despite the fact that they were practically the only people in the shop, Jake managed to throw a diva-style fit.

"How do people do this?" he growled, impatiently drumming with his fingers on the table. "It's agony. How long have we been here?"

Oliver looked at his watch. "Well, in one minute, it'll be exactly a minute and a half."

Miley, meanwhile, was nervously waiting at the counter. She'd been so desperate to get Jake his ice cream that she'd asked a little girl for cutsies. "Thanks for letting me cut in front of you, sweetie," she told the girl as she picked up her tray of sundaes from the counter. "My boyfriend just got his tonsils out. He can barely talk."

"Honey!" Jake yelled at the top of his lungs. "What's taking so long?"

"Did I say *tonsils*?" Miley asked the girl, quickly trying to cover her flub. "I meant kidney." And she hurried off.

Miley figured that the sweeter she acted, the harder it would be for Jake to flip out. "There you go," she said cheerily, placing the tray on the table. "Just what you ordered."

"Is it all better now?" Oliver asked in a mock mommy voice that showed just how tired of the whole thing he was. He'd wanted pizza.

"Totally," Jake said, nodding. It was hard to tell whether he didn't get the fact that Oliver was being sarcastic or just didn't care enough to respond.

"And doesn't it taste much better knowing that you had to wait for it?" Miley asked.

Jake looked at her as if she were nuts. "Not really," he said. Then, raising his voice for the benefit of everyone else in the place, he added, "Um, you know, this ice cream is making me *thirsty*."

"Oh, boy," said Miley, gulping. She knew what was coming next.

Jake held out his hand, waiting for a free drink. But nothing happened. Apparently, he'd forgotten he was still disguised as Milos. He raised his voice a little more. "I said, this ice cream is making me—"

Miley shook her head as she stuffed his mouth full of ice cream. This was going to be a lot harder than she had thought. "Normal people get their own water," she patiently reminded him.

"Really?" Jake swallowed. He seemed genuinely shocked. He casually snatched a bottle of water off a little girl's tray. It was the same little girl Miley had cut in front of on line. "Thanks, kid," Jake said offhandedly. "See ya at the movies."

But the little girl wasn't going to take this one lying down. "Mommy!" she screamed at the top of her lungs.

Miley cringed and sank down in her seat. Could they ever go anywhere, she wondered, without making a scene?

Chapter Four

Miley's evening went from bad to worse. After having ice cream, she and Jake and Lilly and Oliver hung out on the beach, which did put Jake in a decidedly better mood since he didn't have to wait for anything. The thing was, being in a good mood for Jake meant talking— endlessly—about himself!

"So, how'd you get into acting?" Lilly asked, just making conversation. A one-sentence answer would have been fine. But Jake decided to start at the beginning—the *very* beginning. He told them how a modeling agent had spotted him in his stroller when he was five months old, how he'd rocked the first audition he'd ever had, how he had become the face of Wonder Diapers and then the spokesbaby for Natural Baby's Organic Pureed Pineapple Pilaf, and had sent sales flying through the roof. By the time Jake got to his toddler years, Oliver's and Lilly's eyes looked as though they were about to roll back into their heads.

Maybe Jake just had the jitters, Miley thought. Aside from her father and brother, Lilly and Oliver were the most important people in her life. So maybe Jake was talking so much because he was nervous about making a good impression.

Of course, as Jake launched into part

two of *A Star Is Born: The Preschool Years,*
Miley was pretty sure that Oliver and Lilly
were both sleeping.

She let her head drop into her hands.
Lucky them.

Hours later, Miley, Lilly, and Oliver
trudged wearily into the Stewarts' beach
house. They were totally spent. Meanwhile,
an invigorated Jake bounded in after them.

"What a rush!" he whooped. "All night
and no one recognized me. And I've got to
admit, I wasn't sure I could do this normal
thing. I mean, I've been famous since I was
the face of Wonder Diapers—"

"'The only diaper endorsed by astro-
nauts,'" Miley, Oliver, and Lilly recited
together from memory.

"Did I tell you that already?" Jake
asked, surprised.

Miley rolled her eyes. "You might have mentioned it once or twice."

"Or thirty times," Lilly added under her breath.

Strangely, Jake didn't recall having told them any of it. He scratched his head and shrugged. "Anyway, it was a great night," he said. "Except for this wig. I mean, it's worse than the one I wore in *Teen Bigfoot*." And, just in case they didn't know the movie, he rattled off the slogan: *"The only thing bigger than his foot—"*

"Was his heart," Miley, Lilly, and Oliver chorused.

"It still gets to me," Jake said, choking up.

"It's getting to all of us," Miley said snidely.

But Jake didn't seem to notice that Miley's tone was less than kind. "Where can I take this off?" he asked, motioning to his wig.

"Upstairs," Miley told him. "First door on the left."

Jake winked at her. "Be right back."

Miley forced a smile. "Can't wait," she said.

No sooner had the door to the bathroom closed, though, than Lilly and Oliver were on her case. "Uh, Miley, we don't exactly know how to tell you this," Lilly said, frowning, "but—"

"Jake's horrible!" Miley exclaimed.

"Yeah," Lilly said, nodding. "That's pretty much it."

Miley frowned and shook her head. "I don't understand. I mean, Hannah Montana is a star, too. But underneath, Hannah is a real person. Underneath, Jake is just . . ."

"More Jake," said Oliver.

Miley sighed. She thought about saying, "Maybe he was just nervous." But she knew that Lilly and Oliver wouldn't buy it for a second. And honestly, she didn't know if she did, either.

It seemed after tonight that Miley had been right to have all those misgivings. Jake wasn't really the person she'd thought he was at all. "I really liked him," she said sadly. "How could I not see this?"

"None of us saw it," Lilly said, trying to comfort her. "So, what are you going to do?"

Miley bit her lip, uncertain. "Learn to love his flaws?"

Oliver nipped that idea in the bud, though. "Right," he snapped. "Like the adorable way he steals water from little girls."

Miley cringed. The little girl's howls still echoed in her ears. "I have to break up with him, don't I?" she said.

Lilly nodded matter-of-factly. "I think so," she told her.

"What if he gets mad?" said Oliver suddenly. "He could tell your secret."

Miley hadn't considered that. "Guys, come on," she said, waving the awful idea away. "Jake is a lot of things, but he's not evil."

Just then, as if on cue, Jake came down the stairs. He had the black wig in one hand and his cell phone in the other. "I'll tell you what," he barked into the receiver. "Next time you people give me an itchy wig, I'll spread the word and put you out of business. People try to mess with Jake Ryan, Jake Ryan plays hardball." He held the phone away from his ear, then flipped the phone shut before the other person could finish pleading for mercy.

Miley, Lilly, and Oliver tried to hide their horror as Jake joined them at the table. "So, what'd I miss?" he asked with a bright, innocent grin.

"Nothing!" they all said at once.

Jake glanced up at the clock. *Zombie High* was about to begin. Where had all the time gone? "Come on," he urged. "Let's watch *me* on TV!"

As Jake lunged for the remote, Miley wondered just how much worse the situation could get.

Chapter Five

While Miley struggled with what to do about Jake, her brother, Jackson, was feeling pretty awesome about the way he had handled his own problem—Rico.

For a while it had seemed as if Rico would stop at nothing to get Jackson and Oliver's secret Cheeze Jerky recipe. He'd tried every trick in the book: setting up secret video cameras in Jackson and Oliver's kitchen, hiring Natasha to disguise herself as a TV producer from the Cooking Channel. But Jackson and Oliver had thwarted his plots every time.

And so, out of ideas and running low on resources, Rico had finally backed down, and Jackson couldn't help feeling proud. Victory, he thought, had never tasted so sweet—or, to be more precise, so crunchy, cheesy, and full of nitrates!

Jackson didn't want to gloat. . . . No, actually, scratch that. He did want, more than anything, to gloat. "Sorry, folks," he announced in a voice he hoped was loud enough for Rico to hear. "We're all sold out. But don't worry, come back tomorrow—there'll be plenty more!"

He glanced across the beach. "That's right, Rico, I'm turnin' 'em away!" The sour look on Rico's face was positively priceless! Jackson smiled. He had to rub it in some more. "And look!" He held up a wad of cash for Rico to see, then loosened his grip so that several dollars wafted off on the breeze. "It's raining money!" he cried.

Rico shook his head grimly, then bitterly skulked off.

Jackson wasn't done yet. "But look!" he cried, dropping down to the sand where the bills had landed. "I'm rolling in money!" He rolled back and forth, laughing uproariously to himself.

He didn't even see when Oliver arrived. "Whatcha doin'?" Oliver asked, smiling.

"Laughing like Rico and rollin' in money. You should try it, dude, it's fun."

Oliver was game. "Cool!" he said, getting lost in the moment. Then, realizing he'd actually come on a mission, he dug into his pockets. "Oh, but first, my mom gave me the receipts for all the supplies she bought, and we have got to settle up."

Back to business, thought Jackson, picking up the stray bills and brushing the sand off his shirt. Of course they had to pay Ms. Oken back. Without her, they'd have been nothing.

A half hour later, reality had sunk in. If they paid Ms. Oken back, they'd *have* nothing! Who knew freeze-dried beef could cost so much? Jackson sighed. He should have known their massive profits were too good to be true.

Oliver had divided the money into two stacks: one large, one teensy.

"Please tell me this big one's for us," Jackson said, wanting to cry because he knew it wasn't true.

"You might want to look away," Oliver warned him.

Jackson closed his eyes as though Oliver were getting ready to rip a bandage off his knee. "Make it quick," he whimpered.

Oliver took the money. Torn between his business partner and his mother, he had, of course, no choice. "Jackson, I—" he began.

"Just go!" Jackson said, waving him off. He gripped the last remaining dollar tightly in his fist. Victory had sure been sweet—and also really, really short-lived.

As for Miley and Lilly, they were still craving some Mushroom-Meatball Spectacular Deep-Dish Surprise. And so, they soon returned to Pizza Bytes together, after a quick stop at the newsstand.

Sadly, Miley knew that flipping through the celebrity tabloids wasn't exactly the best way to get her mind off her problems.

But there was no way she could help it.

"Look how cute Jake is," she sighed. "Why did he have to talk and ruin everything?" She stared longingly at a spread titled *Teen Celebs Are Regular Folk, Too*. Jake looked adorable carrying that bag of groceries. Okay, yeah, the shot was probably faked. Like Jake was going to wait on line for groceries! Still, the way his arm muscles rippled as he gripped the paper bag . . .

"Okay," said Lilly, jotting something in a notebook, "I've been thinking about your problem, and I've got a couple ideas on how to fix it."

"This isn't gonna be something stupid like 'Move to Peru,' is it?" asked Miley.

"No," said Lilly, grimacing. She scratched something off her list.

"Please tell me you don't have 'Face transplant' on there, too," Miley said. Lilly

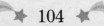

tended to get a few too many ideas from daytime soaps.

"Well . . . I . . ." Lilly sputtered. She crossed one more thing off her shrinking list. "Fine," she grumbled.

Miley appreciated Lilly's attempts to console her. But nothing could make her situation much brighter, she knew. Just being in Pizza Bytes, in fact, was fairly painful. She had to face facts: Jake was a self-obsessed celebrity! Period, end of story. "And now I have got to go to another premiere with him and act like he's not the most obnoxious person I've ever met," Miley moaned. "I just wish I could find a way to get *him* to break up with *me*."

"I know," Lilly agreed. "He'd break up with you in a second if you were half as obnoxious as he is."

Miley suddenly looked up. Hey, she

thought. That was it! *She* could be obnoxious! Well, at least she could pretend to be. "Lilly, you're a genius!"

The weird, poufy white-feather dress with the shoulder strap that looked like the head and neck of a stuffed swan was all Lilly's idea. She'd seen it in a magazine billed as the number one award show wardrobe disaster. Apparently, someone had worn exactly the same outfit to the Oscars one year. What had she been thinking? Miley wondered. She checked out her reflection in the full-length mirror and made a face. The thing was totally atrocious!

If Hannah Montana ever went to the Oscars, an outfit like that would be the last thing she'd ever have worn. But it was perfect for attending a swanky LA movie premiere with Jake. Especially because the entire point of the evening was to get him to break up with her. Wait till he saw her!

Just to be sure, though, Miley and Lilly decided to take the look a step further. In an homage to Jake's beloved *Teen Bigfoot*, and with the help of an old brown shag rug and some wig glue, Lilly gave Miley's underarms a more . . . natural look. Yuck! If *that* didn't turn Jake off, they figured, nothing would.

When Jake's limo driver rang the doorbell, Miley threw on a large overcoat that covered up her outfit. She'd open it when the time was right—preferably in front of a bunch of cameras. Lilly wished her good luck as she headed out the door. Operation Get Jake to Break Up with Me was officially under way.

Chapter Six

Miley probably should have figured that Jake wouldn't notice that the coat she was wearing was unseasonably warm, or that her hair wasn't exactly "styled." In fact, Jake barely noticed anything about her. He ignored her throughout the entire limo ride! First he took a call from his publicist. Then he got a text from his agent. Then a producer called about doing some reshoots. Miley, meanwhile, fidgeted uncomfortably in her swan dress. Did its beak *have* to keep poking her in the the neck?

When they finally arrived at the premiere, a team of hairstylists and makeup people descended on Jake's limo. It seemed Jake had to be prepped one last time before hitting the red carpet. The stylists each climbed into the limo, not even bothering to acknowledge that Miley was there. Actually, one makeup assistant did say, "Hi." The only thing was, she called her Milly.

Apparently this was going to be the theme for the night. "And here comes Jake Ryan," good old Brian Winters announced as they headed down the red carpet, "with his not-famous girlfriend, Milkey!"

"Uh, it's Miley," Jake corrected him. Miley glanced at him for a second. She was surprised he'd even bothered.

Brian Winters shrugged. Like he cared what her name was! Still, he turned to Miley. "How does it feel to be a regular girl dating a big star?" he asked.

Miley took a huge breath. This was it. Her moment had come. "Hang on a sec, Bri," Miley drawled in her thickest Southern accent. "I got a throat itch." She loudly coughed and gagged, as if trying to dislodge a giant gob of phlegm. Jake stared at her, startled.

"Almost," Miley went on, hacking away. At last, she let out a megacough, spraying spit all over the place. "Much better!" she said, feigning relief. Then she turned to Brian, grinning. "You were saying?"

Brian Winters looked completely grossed out as he wiped Miley's spit from his face. "Wow, Jake, this one's a keeper," he said, his lip curling.

"Yes, Brian," a bewildered Jake replied.

Out of the corner of her eye, Miley could see Jake's *Teen Gladiators* costar, Marissa Hughes, coming down the carpet toward them. Miley knew she needed to act quickly, before the cameras moved to her.

"Man, these lights are warm!" Miley declared, fanning herself. "I've just got to air myself out." She unbuttoned her overcoat. It was time for the big reveal. . . .

"Bam!" she exclaimed.

"Wow!" exclaimed Brian Winters at the sight of Miley's swan dress. "I guess we now know what happened to the ugly duckling!"

Jake's jaw, meanwhile, had dropped. He was no longer bewildered. He was stunned. "You know, maybe we should just go inside," he said quickly, trying to pull Miley's overcoat back up around her.

"That's a good idea," Miley told him. "But first I gotta . . ." She raised her arms so that her *Teen Bigfoot*–inspired armpits were fully exposed. "Oh, yeah, that feels nice," she said.

"Wow!" Brian Winters exclaimed again, this time crinkling his nose. "Does anyone have a lawn mower?"

Miley happily watched the scraggly hairs flutter in the wind. "There's a breeze in *Pitts*burgh, if you catch my drift," she said. Lilly had come up with that one, and Miley had to bite her lip to keep from laughing out loud.

"Put your arms down," Jake muttered under his breath.

"Why?" Miley asked, pretending not to know the reason. She peered down at her armpits. "Oh! Oh, man, that's embarrassing," she said with a self-conscious giggle. "I meant to braid those."

"Oh, my gosh," Jake said. "I just forgot we have to feed the cats." He put his hands on her shoulders. "Let's go home," he said, trying to steer her away.

Miley grinned with satisfaction. "You don't have a cat, you silly goose!" She hit him playfully in the chest with the swan head hanging from her shoulder. He was *so* ready to break up with her now—she could tell.

"Maybe we can build one," Jake said, "out of your armpits!"

Mission accomplished, thought Miley, as he dragged her back to the limo. Operation Get Jake to Break Up with Me had most definitely been a success.

Chapter Seven

Miley was certain that Jake would break up with her on the ride home. In fact, she was even surprised he was giving her a ride home. After her performance on the red carpet, she had been sure she'd get ditched at the theater. She'd brought money for cab fare, just in case. So it was downright kindhearted, she thought, of Jake to give her a ride in his limousine. Though, knowing him, he was probably just doing it to protect his career. If he'd broken up with her at the theater, she might have caused another scene, and the paparazzi would have been all over them.

But then, why didn't he break up with her in the limo? she wondered. And then, when they got back to her house, why did he get out of the car and walk her to the front door? What, exactly, was he thinking?

Finally, Miley said something. "Jake, you haven't said a word the whole ride home. Did I do something wrong?"

"Oh, stop it," Jake told her. "I know exactly what you're doing."

He did? "You do?"

"Yeah, of course I do. I'm not an idiot," he said.

Oh, so he knew she wanted him to break up with her. He was just drawing the night out to torture her. Nice. "Okay, fine,"

Miley told him, "maybe I went about it the wrong way, but—"

Jake interrupted her. "Little Miss Hannah Montana can't handle it when it's all about Jake Ryan."

"What?" Miley gasped, taken aback.

"Yeah!" Jake snapped. "You'll do anything to steal my spotlight. Face it, you're jealous of me."

"Jealous of you?" Miley couldn't believe this guy. That was the most preposterous thing she'd ever heard, and she was about to tell him just that when it suddenly dawned on her . . . Why bother? If that was what he thought, fine. This was as good a way out as any other.

"Why, yes, I am," she declared. "I *am* a jealous egomaniac, and you should dump me right now. You know what? I'll make it easier on you." She went inside the house.

"Good-bye!" she said, slamming the door behind her.

Before she could lock it, however, Jake followed her in. "I'm not going to break up with you," he said.

He wasn't? *Dang!* Miley said under her breath.

"Miley, we can get through this. You'll learn not to be jealous, just like I learned to be a normal guy."

"Oh, sweet niblets!" Miley exclaimed in exasperation. She realized she was going to have to do this the hard way. She took a deep breath and looked Jake straight in the eye. "You don't know what a normal guy is," she said.

"What're you talking about?" Jake argued. "Okay, maybe I'm not normal on the outside." Miley rolled her eyes. Even in the heat of a breakup, Jake was thinking about his good looks. "But inside beats the heart of a kid just like you!"

Wait a second, Miley thought. "That's from *Teen Bigfoot!*" she said.

"So?" Jake held up his hands. He didn't see what the big deal was.

"*So?*" Miley exclaimed. "That's exactly what I'm talking about. Normal people don't say things other people wrote for them! Normal people don't steal water from *little girls!*"

"Excuse me if I didn't know that!" Now Jake really looked mad. "The only reason I did this stupid 'normal' thing was for you. You know what? I'm out of here," he said.

Finally! thought Miley. Except now, she was too enraged to let him have the last word. "Being normal is not stupid," she retorted. "It lets me have real friends. And it reminds me that I'm just like everybody else."

"And you like that?" Jake said.

"I love that. And I thought you did, too. Remember when we met, you said sometimes you wish you had a normal life? Where's that guy? That's the guy I want for a boyfriend."

Jake suddenly looked thoughtful. "Well, if you didn't want to go out with me anymore, why didn't you just tell me, instead of going all"—he pointed to her armpits—"woolly mammoth at the premiere?"

"Because I was afraid if I dumped you, you'd get so upset and you'd . . ." Miley paused and bit her lip.

"What?" Jake asked. "Tell your secret?" Miley shrugged, and Jake's face fell. "Well, if that's the kind of guy you think I am, then maybe I *will* tell your secret."

And with that, he left.

Chapter Eight

There was an old song Mr. Stewart sang. Jackson didn't know the exact lyrics. Something about knowing when to hold, and knowing when to fold, and knowing when to walk away . . . The song was about poker. Knowing when to fold meant understanding the game was over.

It was no coincidence, then, that that very song was going through Jackson's head the next morning as he disassembled

Jackson and Oliver's Cheeze Jerky Shack. It was time to fold. Still, Jackson didn't walk away. Rather, he walked across the sand to Rico's and got behind the counter.

No one was more surprised to see him there than Rico. "What are you doing here?" he demanded.

"What are you talking about?" Jackson asked. "I work here."

"But I fired you."

"No, you didn't."

"Sure I did. And then you opened that shack."

"What shack?"

Rico turned to look at Jackson's shack. But nothing was there. Was he going crazy? "But it was right over . . . and you . . . and Oliver . . . and Cheeze Jerky . . . and I was in a baby stroller . . ."

Jackson felt a little bad for the guy. Then

again, Rico had set him up, then tried to steal from him. Plus, he charged three dollars for water! He deserved to think he was going crazy for a little bit.

"It will be okay," Jackson said gently, putting his hand on Rico's shoulder. "Let me take you home."

Back at the Stewarts' beach house, Miley was deep down in the dumps, and her father was trying to cheer her up the best way he knew how.

"Here you go, darlin'," he said, handing her a bowl of ice cream. "Fudge ripple's like a heartbreak airbag. It doesn't stop the hurtin', but it cushions the blow."

Miley sadly jabbed at the heaping scoop with her spoon. "I don't get it," she said. "I lie to my boyfriend and feel horrible. I tell him the truth and it blows up in my face.

Maybe I should just give up guys for good."

"Don't be so hard on yourself," said Mr. Stewart, even though he secretly liked the idea of Miley giving up guys for a while. "It wasn't the truth or the lies that caused all this. It was the boy. He just wasn't the right one."

"I guess you're right," said Miley. "But you know what's weird? Now that Jake's going to blow my secret, I don't know which I'm going to miss more, my normal life, or the guy I thought Jake was."

Mr. Stewart sighed. He was just as worried as Miley. If this Jake boy told her secret, *all* their lives would change. As Hannah Montana's family, he and Jackson would have to say good-bye to their normal lives. Still, he decided not to share his worries with Miley. Why make it worse for her? "Well, honey," he said consolingly, "no matter what happens, we're going to make it through this. We always do."

He heard a voice from the front porch. "Hello? Delivery for Miley Stewart."

"Back here!" Mr. Stewart shouted.

The familiar delivery guy from the flower shop appeared and handed Miley a long silver box topped with a big gold bow.

"Now, who would be sending you flowers?" Mr. Stewart asked.

Miley opened the card and let her dad read it over her shoulder.

Dear Miley,
    I thought about what you said, and you're right. I do wish I was a normal person sometimes. I just don't know how to do that yet.

But when I figure it out, I hope I'll be worthy of someone as terrific as you. And don't worry, your secret will always be safe with me.

Love,
Leslie

"Who the Sam heck is Leslie?" asked Mr. Stewart, scratching his chin.

Miley opened the box. Inside was a single red rose.

"A friend," she answered, with a happy, mysterious grin. "A very good friend."

Put your hands together for the next Hannah Montana book . . .

Reality Check

Adapted by N. B. Grace

Based on the series created by Michael Poryes and Rich Correll & Barry O'Brien

Based on the episode, "Song Sung Bad," Written by Ingrid Escajeda

Part Two is based on the episode, "Sleepwalk This Way," Written by Heather Wordham

Lilly's got the perfect gift for her mom: she's recording her a song! The only trouble is, her singing voice isn't so sweet. Miley decides to pitch in and secretly lends her dazzling Hannah Montana vocals to the recording. When Lilly hears the song, she is psyched and decides to challenge awful Amber to a singing competition. Will Miley be able to rescue her friend from major embarrassment? Or will Lilly's performance hit a low note?